FATHER CHRISTMAS

NEEDS A WEE!

Nicholas Allan

Red Fox

Father Christmas needs a wee,
He's been drinking drinks since half past three!

At number 1 . . .

ONE hot choc, yum!

TWO plates of stew.

At number 3
THREE cups of tea,

At number 4
he'd had FOUR more!

At number 5
FIVE pops
(with pies!),

fruit mix (all SIX).

At number 7 milk,

SEVEN, pure heaven!

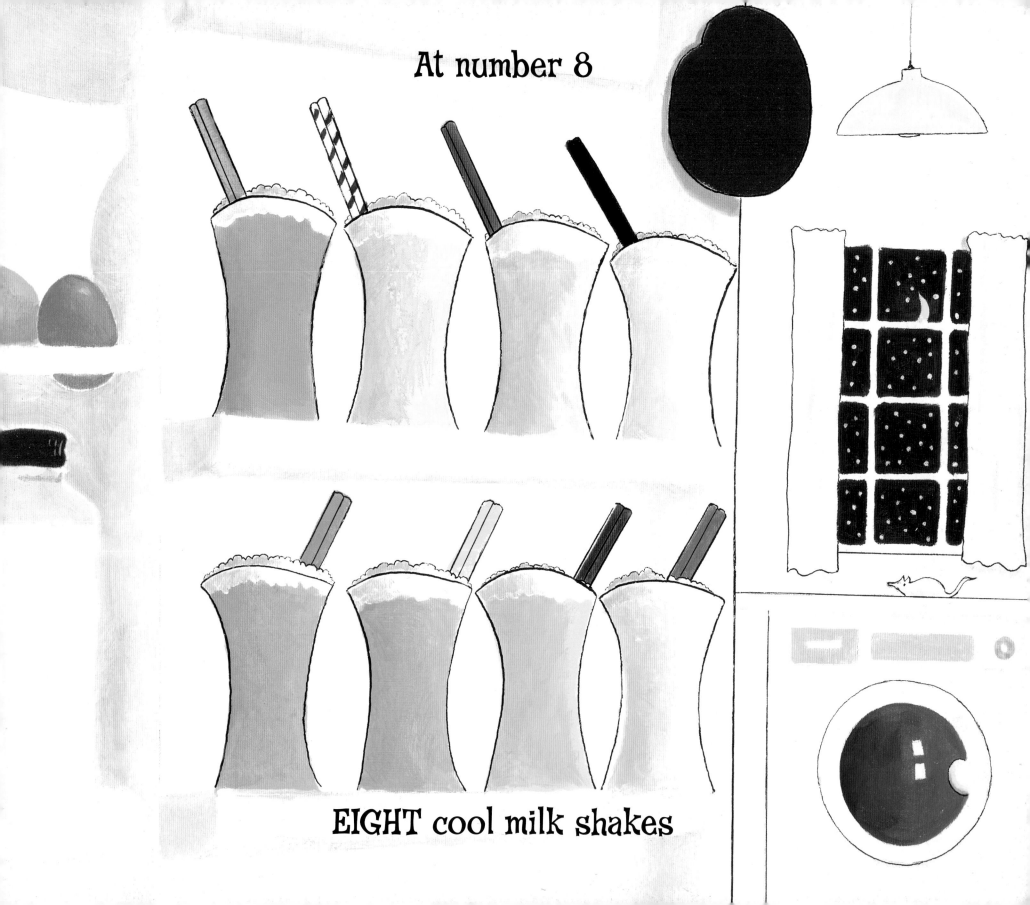

At number 8

EIGHT cool milk shakes

At number 9

NINE lemon and limes.

TEN teas . . . and THEN . . .

I think that you will clearly see

Why Father Christmas needs a wee!

But, oh! What with all those drinks in mind . . . .

he forgot to leave the presents behind! And SO . . . .

At number 10 he left TEN pens,

At number 9 NINE nursery rhymes.

At number 8 EIGHT pairs of skates,

At number 7 sweets! SEVEN, *more* heaven!

At number 6 SIX colourful bricks,

At number 5 FIVE toys to drive.

At number 4 FOUR beasts that ROAR!

At number 3 THREE Christmas trees.

At number 2 TWO cows that . . .

MOOOOOO!

And so, at last, his work is do

And now it's time for him to flee,

For Father Christmas needs a wee!

Through the town, across the sky,
The sledge it rises, rises high!

Above the clouds and over the sea,
He must be quick, he needs his wee!

At last he's back, at home, all safe,

Just *look* at that smile upon his face!

He feels in his pocket - but *where* is the key?
For Father Christmas NEEDS A WEE!

An elf with a gift appears by the door,

"I found this key – just here, on the floor."

He thanks the elf, and turns the lock,

He runs up the stairs, right up to the top.

And there is the loo, he shuts the door . . .

For Y.

FATHER CHRISTMAS NEEDS A WEE
A RED FOX BOOK 978 1 862 30825 1

First published in Great Britain by Red Fox,
an imprint of Random House Children's Books
A Random House Group Company

This edition published 2009

3 5 7 9 10 8 6 4

Red Fox Books are published by Random House Children's Books,
61–63 Uxbridge Road, London W5 5SA

www.kidsatrandomhouse.co.uk
www.nicholasallan.co.uk
www.rbooks.co.uk

Addresses for companies within The Random House Group Limited can be found at: www.randomhouse.co.uk/offices.htm

THE RANDOM HOUSE GROUP Limited Reg. No. 954009

A CIP catalogue record for this book is available from the British Library.

Printed in Italy

This book belongs to

TALIA Be
....